My Grandmother's
Dragon

D. D. McDee

HUGO HOUSE PUBLISHERS, LTD.

My Grandmother's Dragon

ISBN: 978-1-948261-44-9

Library of Congress Control:

Illustrator: Aulysh

Cover Design & Interior Layout: Ronda Taylor, www.HeartWorkCreative.com

Hugo House Publishers, Ltd.
Austin, TX • Denver, CO
www.HugoHousePublishers.com

Dedication

To my real-life Grandmother, Birdine Crawford. She wanted ten kids, had five, and was truly passionate about education. After she sent the last of her children off to college, she drove two hundred miles, round trip *every day*, to get her teaching degree. One of her classes was even taught by one of her sons. She became a high-school English teacher and loved every minute of it. She was an amazing woman and would have handled dragons brilliantly, as she did everything else.

Prologue

I was raised by parents who didn't believe in talking down to their children. They used their normal vocabulary around us, and being readers, they both knew many words. When they used a word around us that we didn't know, they always took the time to define it for us, which was great. Consequently, I learned to love words and their usage. There are so many incredible words in the English language, it seems a shame to only use some of them.

There are some words the just roll off the tongue and others that are incredible because they mean such a specific thing. For instance there is a word that means a fear of the number thirteen. The word is **triskaidekaphobia.** That word is not only very specific, but boy does it roll off the tongue once you learn how to say it. It's even more fun when you get to use it, correctly, in a sentence!

If you notice on the front cover, I have added a trigger warning: "This book contains big words and rural Texas attitudes." The rural Texas attitudes are yours to accept—or not.

Now, a bit more about those "big" words. Although I wrote this book for young adults, I used the words I normally use. I have included a glossary to define the words that may be unfamiliar. If you run across a word you don't understand, and it's not in the glossary, try looking it up. The Collins Cobuild online dictionary (or the actual book if you come across one), is one of my favorites. I encourage you to use it a lot.

I hope that those who read my book learn to love words as much as I do. And I sincerely hope you enjoy the story.

Deanne Macdonald, a.k.a D.D. McDee

Chapter 1

There are two things I'll always remember about my grandmother. She could take a place that is as close to Hell as one can come without actually dying and turn it into a wonderful place to be. And boy, could she handle dragons. Well dragon. One, to be exact.

Grandma lived in a little town on the plains of Texas that, as far as I could tell, never should have existed at all. Most towns are rooted near a river or a lake or some sort of natural beauty. Not so this town. Spearman lies smack dab in the middle of nowhere.

I sometimes think that it must have been founded when some hot, weary, foot-sore pioneer woman had finally had enough. I imagine it going something like this: "That's it! I am not taking another step! You can just build me a house right here!"

"But Honey—"

"Don't you Honey me. I've walked hundreds of miles in this ridiculous heat. I'm dirty, I'm tired, and I'm dead serious. NOT ANOTHER STEP!" And thus the town was born.

If you aren't from these parts, it's hard to describe these wide-open plains that were once called the Great American Desert. Look in any direction and all you see is flat, dry, brown-looking dirt which supports crops only when they're grown with extreme patience and enough water to support a medium-sized city for a year. The winters are cold and windy. The spring is dry and windy. The summers are hot and windy, and the fall is just plain windy. In fact when the wind stops, you had better start looking for a storm cellar because it means a tornado is about to remove the roof of your house and deposit it in the next county. In fact this town is so windy that it has a windmill museum at the edge of town—really. You can google it. https://texasplainstrail.com/plan-your-adventure/historic-sites-and-cities/sites/jb-buchanan-vintage-windmill-collection.

Thunderstorms are another thing that makes living anywhere in this region a real adventure. After looking into the black clouds of a real Texas thunderstorm as it moves across the open prairie toward you, flashing lightning every second or two, you can honestly tell your friends that you've looked into the maw of disaster and survived. If you're driving when the sirens that signal an approaching thunderstorm go off, you immediately high tail it for the nearest low piece of ground, which is quite a trick in country where the land varies about a foot in elevation every two or three hundred miles. If

Chapter 1

the lightning doesn't strike you, the water that pours from the sky and swirls around will get you. It turns streets into rivers that steal anything smaller than a Chevy pickup and place them somewhere else, preferably someone's basement. (And you thought Texans drove pickups because they looked good.)

Now you might think that my grandma's house would be the last place in the world I'd want to spend my summers (especially considering that in the summer if the temperature drops below 109 degrees, it's considered a cold snap) but that just isn't so. I loved to visit my grandma. She was a very unique individual. She was the kind of grandmother every child should have. Everything she did was touched with just a little bit of magic, a fact that children all over the town were aware of. Her house sometimes looked like the local playground, what with the number of kids who were always around, helping her with something or other or just stopping by to visit and have cookies and milk. So it was no great surprise that they came to her when they started having trouble with the dragon.

Chapter 2

I'll never forget the day that Johnnie Tyler, Mary Beth Watson and Annie Johnson came over to lay the problem exactly where it belonged—right in my grandmother's lap. I'd been down to the Five and Dime (yes, they still called them that back then—they probably still do in Texas) and I walked in mid-explanation. Johnnie was talking, the girls were looking on and nodding every now and then, and Grandma was listening intently. This looked really interesting, so I quietly made my way to the kitchen counter and perched myself on it.

Johnnie glanced my way and continued, "… The next thing that turned up missing was the gold ball on top of the school."

I gave Grandma a sort of curious look and she gave me her shut-up-and-pay-attention look. She'd worked on that look when she first became a teacher, and it worked like a charm. I didn't say a word, and boy was I paying attention.

"At first," Johnnie continued, "everybody thought Bobby Lee was doing it, but he couldn't have been the one because he'd been over to Harley Simpson's farm for three days. So me and the girls decided to find out who it was."

I could see my grandma itching to say, "The girls and I" but for once she didn't correct Johnnie's ever-atrocious grammar.

"We figured that whoever took the ball from the school and the eagle off the courthouse couldn't possibly pass up the big globe on top of the bank. So we sat up all night and—" Johnnie hesitated for a long time before he finished that particular sentence. "—and around about three o'clock in the morning, well, that's when we seen him. The girls were asleep, so I woke 'em up, and they seen him too." He looked at the girls for confirmation, and they energetically shook their heads in the affirmative.

"We knew we couldn't go to the sheriff," Annie added. "He'd think we'd all gone crazy or was just playing practical jokes or something." Grandma nodded her understanding, and I began to feel a little disoriented with all that nodding going on.

My grandma tilted her head a bit, thought it over for a minute and said, "So, I take it from the fact that you came here that y'all want me to go find this dragon and do something about him." Grandma had a nasty habit of getting right to the point.

"Yes ma'am," they all three replied together.

Grandma sighed and leaned back in her chair. "Okay, just for the sake of argument, let's say we find the dragon, and I go in to have a chat with him. What on God's green Earth makes

y'all think that this dragon of yours won't just have me for an afternoon snack?"

The children looked horrified. "He wouldn't dare!" protested Annie.

"He isn't **our** dragon," added Mary Beth.

Then Johnnie threw in the kicker, "We know where he lives." After that there was dead silence from everyone else in the room. Johnnie waited a bit and said, "He lives down in the brakes about a mile this side of the graveyard."

For those of you who don't know what brakes are, these kind of brakes aren't the things that are put in your car to stop it. In north Texas, the brakes are actually a rip in the earth that's filled with dry brush and stunted trees. They run for miles and even sometimes have water in them (for instance in the middle of the aforementioned thunderstorms).

Grandma waited for a long time, just looking at the children and thinking. I think it was Annie's whisper that finally decided her. There was so much pleading in her voice as she said, "Mrs. Crawford, you gotta help us. We're afraid."

Grandma stood up, reached back, untied her apron and said, "Okay, we'll go see if we can find this dragon. You kids go call your parents and tell them I invited y'all for a picnic down at my farm." Just because Grandma taught English at the local high school was no reason for her to stop speaking good old-fashioned Texan. The kids perked right up and darted out of the room to go call their parents. In those days, no one had a cell phone, and Grandma's phone was in the back hall. So that's where they went.

I looked at my grandmother and shook my head. "You don't really think there's a dragon living in the brakes, do you?"

Grandma lifted her apron over her head and hung it on the peg next to the door. "I certainly hope not. But those children saw something, and I think we'd better find out what it is. Make some sandwiches and throw in some of those cookies I baked this morning. I'll go get your granddad's shotgun."

That surprised me. Grandma didn't really like guns and would rather hoe the head off a snake than shoot it. But obviously, a dragon was probably going to require something larger than a hoe.

Chapter 3

It didn't take long to pack the kids, the lunch and the shotgun into the pickup. We had to drive off the highway and over several stretches of open country before we reached the spot Johnnie said the dragon lived. It was rough going, but Grandpa's truck was raised in the country, so it didn't mind.

When we reached the edge of the drop-off where Johnnie insisted the dragon lived, Grandma was all business and orders. "You kids stay here in the pickup with the doors locked. If I'm not back in thirty minutes, y'all get out of here and go tell the sheriff that I've had an accident."

I looked at her with a gleam in my eye. If she thought I was going to miss out on this, she was soon going to have another thought. "Grandma, I don't know how to drive. Besides, I'm going with you."

Grandma's, "No you aren't" almost drowned out Johnnie's "I can drive," but I heard it.

"See Grandma. Johnnie can drive the pickup, and I can go with you."

Grandma gritted her teeth and spat out another *no,*

"Grandma, you always told me that when it comes to stubbornness the Crawfords have more of it than Texas has rattlesnakes and spiders. We are both Crawfords. Now you and I can sit here and argue all day, and I'm still going to follow you down there, so why don't you just take me with you?"

Grandma glared at me for a full minute. I tell you, if looks could kill, I'd have been lying in a coffin after about three seconds. But since I didn't fall dead at her feet, Grandma reluctantly agreed.

We got out of the pickup and Grandma grabbed the shotgun. She checked to make sure it was loaded, and we set off down the slippery slope. Our progress was anything but graceful. We slid part way down on our feet and the rest of the way on our rear ends. Just as I was dusting a goodly portion of Texas countryside off my legs, I heard an electric buzz saw go off right beside me. I froze immediately. Most people think that a rattlesnake sounds something like a happy little tambourine. Anyone who's grown up around the little beasts knows better. It really does sound more like a buzz saw. They can shake that rattle so fast it doesn't sound like a rattle at all.

Grandma turned around faster than an old-time gunslinger and gave that little sucker both barrels at the same time. Little pieces of rattlesnake were instantly blown all over the scenery. Grandma shuddered as she broke open the shotgun and reloaded. "I hate rattlesnakes," she said under her breath. I looked at the little bits of rattlesnake falling all around me and almost laughed at the incongruity of this whole venture.

Chapter 3

Here I was with a woman who hated reptiles (it wasn't just rattlesnakes that she hated) so much that it almost bordered on the absurd, yet here she was out looking for a dragon. If we actually found one, God only knows what she'd do.

I suppressed my giggles and looked at my grandmother. She was still sort of shaking off the effects of seeing the snake. "Well," I said sort of sheepishly, "If there is a dragon down here, we just lost any chance we had of sneaking up on him."

Grandma shot me one of her looks. This one said, "Don't be absurd." Just to make sure I didn't mistake her meaning she said, "Don't be absurd. There's no such thing as a dragon."

Any further conversation at that point would have been useless, so I began looking around for the cave Johnnie said was there. I found it and shouted at my grandmother. She took the lead, and I followed behind with a huge flashlight to light our way.

The inside of the cave was absolutely delightful. It was cool and very quiet. As I played the beam of the flashlight over the walls surrounding us, I noticed a type of rock I'd never seen before. The base layer seemed to be some sort of red clay, but it had rows of gold in what looked like sideways stalagmites. For a moment I wished that my Uncle Mike were here to explain the beautiful formation. Being a geologist, he could have told me exactly what it was, or so I thought.

I walked over to it and was about to touch it when an eye the color of the sky opened up right where I was about to put my hand. I felt just like a rabbit sitting frozen in front of a snake. I couldn't move, and I knew that if I tried to speak my voice would betray me and come out an unintelligible squeak. I blinked several times and tried my best to swallow, but I found that my mouth was as dry as the country around me. I stumbled backwards, opening and closing my mouth and gasping for air like a stranded fish. Finally, I made a sound that a starving kitten would have been embarrassed to have uttered.

Grandma misinterpreted the sound and asked, "Are there rats in here?" as she aimed the shotgun at the floor. Pity the poor rat that might have wandered out of his hole at that moment. Grandma hated rats almost as much as she hated snakes.

I shook my head and managed another squeak while gesturing like a windmill in a high wind in the direction of the dragon.

It was the movement of the dragon's eyelid as he yawned and blinked languorously that finally caught Grandma's attention, but being a little older and less inclined to losing her wits, Grandma did the only thing a sensible Texan would do. She whipped up the shotgun, aimed it right between the dragon's massive eyes, and cocked both hammers.

"Oh please madam, calm yourself." The dragon's voice rang in my head. It took me a moment to digest the fact that not only did he speak English, the kind complete with British accent, but he also did it telepathically and in a truly sexy deep bass voice. The dragon continued in that ever-so proper English tone, *"I've done you no harm, and yet you come bursting into my bedroom, armed with that ridiculous weapon and disturb*

14

my repose. May I kindly ask just what it is that you think you're doing?"

For the first time in my life, I saw my grandmother speechless. It was shocking. This was, after all, the woman who seemed to have a wealth of deliciously clever comments stored in her head just waiting for the right time to pull them out and end an inane conversation in an instant. This was another of the many skills she learned from years of teaching high school kids. Her silence seemed to break the numbness my own mind had been trapped in.

With the somewhat insane bravery of a thirteen-year-old girl, I whirled on the dragon and fixed him with what I hoped was a grand imitation of my Grandmother's famous baleful stare. "What have you done to my grandmother, you horrible beast?" I wanted to use a word much stronger than horrible, but my grandmother would have washed my mouth out with soap (literally) had I done so.

The dragon actually laughed. So much for my baleful stare. *"My, my. I have heard that Texans are feisty, but I sincerely believed the rumors were more than slightly exaggerated. I can see that I was mistaken."* He paused and added in a tone which I would classify as mollifying, *"Young human, I have done nothing to your sweet grandmother, nor would I. I have come to your country only to broaden my horizons, not to eat or in any other way harm the denizens of your interesting land."*

"Oh," I replied in an embarrassed whisper. "In that case," my voice seemed to pick up in volume as my fear started to subside, "I apologize." I hoped the dragon was sincere.

Chapter 3

I decided pretty darn fast that it would be difficult, if not impossible to lie telepathically, so I really was sorry to have upset him or her, whatever it was.

"Your apology was most graciously tendered; therefore, I must graciously accept it," the dragon replied. *"Now madam, since your granddaughter and I have reached a somewhat uneasy truce, would you please lower your weapon? I'm sure if it went off in here it would make a dreadfully loud noise."* Now that had some sincere truth to it.

Grandma uncocked the hammers of the shotgun and lowered the muzzle. "Well, look at that! A real live, honest-to-goodness dragon, right here in Hansford County no less." Grandma cocked her head and looked the dragon over very carefully. "If you really mean me and mine no harm, then I too must apologize. I'm very sorry we disturbed your nap. How about starting this whole conversation over?"

The dragon raised his head, looked my Grandmother over with the same thoroughness with which she had examined him, and smiled. Up until that moment I didn't know that dragons could smile. Actually, not knowing the dragons even existed, I'd have to say that I was completely ignorant of *any* dragon habits or customs. The dragon agreed to my grandmother's suggestion, and we all started over.

Introductions came first followed by an invitation from Hexley B. Whitney Kingsley (also known as dragon-who-loves-to-hear-strange-tales-told-by-humans) to come by and visit any time.

Just after the invitation was tendered, Johnnie, Mary Beth and Annie cautiously crept into the cave. When they saw that Grandma and I were talking to a dragon, their eyes popped open in sheer delight. Johnny let out an awed gasp followed by, "Wow ... cool." The girls emitted little girl squeals, and all three said at once, "Can we pet him?"

Grandma looked at Hexley, who assented with a slight nod of his head. Grandma smiled at the children, "Sure you can pet him. Just don't get too close to his teeth. He might sneeze or something, and you might find yourselves missing a few fingers."

The dragon looked positively insulted. A small plume of smoke escaped from his nose. "*Madam, I would never harm these children. I love children.*" Then he snorted accompanied by another small puff of smoke. "*Besides, dragons don't sneeze.*"

I stored that little tidbit in a brand-new file in my mind entitled "things previously unknown about dragons." That file now had several items of information in it including "dragons don't sneeze" and "at least one dragon speaks telepathically in a British accent." By the end of the summer, that particular mental file had expanded into an entire data bank.

While the children were petting the dragon's armor-plated hide, I sidled over to my grandmother. "Grandma, I think we have a bit of a problem." Grandma looked at me with concern while keeping an eye on the dragon and the children. "Judging by the size of that dragon, he's going to need a lot of food, and I am guessing that dragons are not inclined to be herbivorous. What are we going to do if he starts eating all the cows and sheep in the area? Grandpa could go broke. The whole county might unite and hunt him down."

Grandma frowned and looked at the dragon again. We thought we hadn't been overheard, and we hadn't been. The children were making much too much noise for that. However, we weren't used to the whole telepathic thing, and we soon found out that you can't keep secrets from a dragon. We were in the middle of trying to come up with a solution when Hexley spoke, "*Please do not worry about my dietary habits. Dragons do not need to consume food to live. Magic sustains us. But I do really like sweets. Do you have cookies in the vehicle you came in?*"

"Well, yes I do," my Grandmother replied. "Johnnie, go get the picnic basket from the truck."

Chapter 4

As Johnny ran off to get the cookies, I could see that Grandma was chewing on something. "You said your nickname is dragon-who-likes-to-hear-strange-stories-read-by-humans right?"

Hexley nodded. "*I love stories. I love rip-roaring American adventure stories. English stories are sometimes soooo stuffy. Except for that one fellow. What was his name, oh yes, William— William Shakespeare. He was delightful. 'To be or not to be.' Yes, those are wonderful stories.*"

My sense of the ridiculous suddenly asserted itself, and I found myself starting to giggle. The sight of a beast the size of a small train, with eyes as big as the hubcaps on my Grandfather's pickup, whose teeth could probably crush a refrigerator with the greatest of ease—this great beast quoting Shakespeare was just too much. The giggle grew like a crack in a dam and spilled over into unrestrained laughter. Grandma frowned somewhat worried that my laughter would insult Hexley. But he knew why I was laughing. He seemed a bit puzzled by it all, but he was not insulted. We had something he wanted—stories read to him by humans.

My grandmother also had something she wanted. Children who could read better. At heart, she was and always would be a teacher, like her mother before her and several of her children. Teaching seems to run in the Crawford blood.

Once I got my giggles under control, she eyed the dragon carefully, and I could see the horse-trader in her coming out. She had a plan, all she had to do was sell it to the Dragon.

"Hexley, how would you feel about coming on over and living with us at our farm? I'll bring you children who will read to you." She paused before adding in the kicker. "And … you can have as many cookies to eat as you wish." Grandma then told him that if he stayed at the farm, he could also listen to music, watch TV and discover some new things to do. He liked the music idea, but TV held no real interest to him.

After carefully contemplating her offer, Hexley said, *"Well madam, that is the best offer I have received in several hundred years. I have considered it, and I do believe I will accept it but with a bit of a revision. I will visit the farm, but I like my cave. It's cool and quiet and the wind doesn't blow in here."*

After they agreed, Hexley did make one request. He wanted to see some American movies. This was the first time I got an inkling of the kind of logistics I might have to handle in the future if I were to have dragons as friends. It sounded easy enough until we realized that he was too large to fit in the movie theatre—not to mention a little too conspicuous. However, problems are made to be solved, and that's just what we did. Since Spearman, Texas boasted a lovely drive-in movie theatre, we just disguised him as a cool sculpture and placed him in the back row. He enjoyed himself immensely. Only the children knew he was real. I think that was part of the fun.

So Hexley came to the farm regularly, where grandma brought the local children under the guise of English tutoring. None of the grownups in town actually knew that Hexley was the tutor, so to speak. She couldn't teach him to read because the print in the books was too small, and he couldn't quite get his claws to turn the pages. But he loved the stories. The children not only became great readers, they actually fought over who would get to read the next story, which pleased my grandmother no end.

And that's how my grandmother handled the dragon. She even read to him—the more advanced stories, but eventually her students were able to handle the big stuff.

It was the best summer ever! We even disguised Hexley as a homecoming parade float, so he could visit the town in the daylight. He won first prize!

But like many good things, Hexley's visit came to an end. When the cold north winds of winter came ripping across the plains, Hexley said his goodbyes and headed for warmer climes. Sometimes when I think about him hard enough, he'll answer up and tell me that he's doing fine, sort of a telepathic post card. He's somewhere in the Caribbean now. Maybe I'll take a cruise and pack up some books to read to him. I don't know. For now, it's enough to know that he's alive and well and thriving on stories of pirates and voodoo magic.

About the Author

D.D. McDee comes from a long line of interesting women who wrote wonderful things. Her great grandmother was a poet, her grandmother (the one this story was written about) was a farmwife, a writer and high school teacher, and her mother wrote epic letters that were each one an adventure story. After writing stories in her head for years, DD finally started putting them down in her computer. This is the first she's gotten published.

Acknowledgments

I want to give a warm shout out to my illustrator Aulysh. I found him online, and he lives in Indonesia. It was interesting trying to get someone who lives in a lush tropical environment to understand just what the plains of Texas look like. He did an awesome job and I feel he added a wonderfully magical quality to the artwork.

Glossary

Absurd: Impossible to take seriously, silly

Accompanied by: Goes with

Affirmative: Agreeing with a statement or request

Aforementioned: Something that you talked about or mentioned before

Asserted: To say something forcefully

Atrocious: Really bad, not good at all

Baleful: Threatening h5arm

Besides: used to emphasize an additional point that you are making, especially one that you consider to be important.

Broaden my horizons: Increase the range of your knowledge, understanding or experience.

Buzz Saw: A power saw for cutting wood or metal consisting of a toothed disk rotated at high speed.

Caribbean: An area that contains many beautiful islands that is south of the US and east of Central America. Many people go there for vacation.

Confirmation: Saying that something is for sure true.

Consequently: as a result.

Consume: To eat or use up.

Conspicuous: standing out so that you are clearly visible.

Contemplating: thinking about whether or not to do something

Denizens: The people, plants or animals that live in a particular place.

Dietary: anything that concerns a person's diet.

Digest: To understand information when there is a lot of it or it is difficult or unexpected.

Disoriented: Confused. Unable to think clearly or make good decisions.

Dreadfully: Very, extremely

Elevation: How high land is based on how far above sea level you are.

Emitted: To make a sound

Exaggerated: Described something in a way that makes it seem better, worse, larger, more important, etc., than it really is.

Feisty: Lively, determined and courageous. It can also mean touchy and likely to attack.

Five and Dime: A store selling a wide variety of inexpensive household and personal goods. Like the big-box store before big-box stores were invented.

Graciously: in a very pleasant and mannerly way.

Herbivorous: Eating plants as opposed to eating meat.

Hightail it: To go as fast as possible, especially when running away

Honest-to-goodness: Genuine and real

Horrified: Very shocked or frightened

Ignorant: Not knowing something

Immensely: To a very large degree

Inane: Very silly or stupid

Inclined: Feeling that you want to do something

Incongruity: Something that seems strange when considered together with the other things that are happening.

Itching to: Wanting to do something very much.

Languorously: In a way that shows you are feeling pleasantly relaxed or tired.

Literally: Describing something the way it really is even though it may seem surprising, not made to sound or look bigger or different than it is.

Maw: Something that seems to open up and suck you in completely.

Previously: at some time before the period that you are talking about

Proposition: An offer or suggestion.

Put forth: To set before one for a decision.

Reluctantly: In a hesitant way. Not totally willing.

Repose: A state of rest or sleep.

Reptiles: Animals like snakes, lizards, crocodiles, and turtles.

Sake of argument: As a place to start a discussion

Sheepishly: Looking slightly embarrassed because you feel foolish or you have done something silly.

Sincere: Like you are saying something that you really mean.

Smack dab: Exactly, precisely.

Stalagmites: A long piece of rock that sticks up from the floor of a cave. Stalagmites are formed by the slow dropping of water containing the mineral lime.

Subside: To go down to a lower or the normal level.

Telepathically: In a way that directly sends and receives thoughts to and from another, without words or gestures.

Tendered: To formally offer or give something to another.

Unrestrained: Not held back—uncontrolled.

Voodoo: A type of magic or witchcraft practiced in the Caribbean. The idea of zombies came from Voodoo originally.

Y'all: Southern for all you people that I am speaking to

Uneasy: Slightly nervous, worried or upset about something.

Unintelligible: Impossible to understand

Unrestrained: not held back

www.ingramcontent.com/pod-product-compliance
Lightning Source LLC
Chambersburg PA
CBHW041032170626
46815CB00005B/296